What's All the Commotion?

A Book about Social Distancing

Written by Jessie Glenn   Illustrated by Kevin King

Eldredge Books

Portland, Oregon

What's All the Commotion? A Book about Social Distancing

Eldredge Books, Portland, OR 97290
© 2019 by Jessie Glenn

ISBN: 978-0-9977491-4-4

www.eldredgebooks.com

Dedicated to Indigo and Juniper,

who told me there needed to be a book about "the commotion."

Most everyone knows, when you sneeze or cough: cover your nose!

Most everyone knows that you should wash your hands: often!

Most everyone knows that when you're sick, you should stay home until you are better.

But *why* do people stay home when they're sick?

We stay home so that we don't pass on the kind of germs that spread illness from one person to another.

Did *you* know that?

Do *you* have any questions about germs and how they spread?

At the beginning of 2020, a lot of people around the world started hearing about a new type of virus that has created a lot of commotion.

What have *you* heard about the commotion?

Some illnesses, including this new virus, can be passed on from sneezing and coughing and touching things that people who are sick have touched.

This virus is passed along quickly. It is more contagious than many colds and flus. Sadly, many people have gotten sick.

Many doctors and nurses and other workers are helping to care for people who have gotten sick.

Happily, most children do not get very sick from this illness.

But some people can get very sick.

Is there anyone *you* are worried about right now?

The best way for us all to take care of each other at the same time is to social distance.

What's social distance mean?

Social distance means, as much as possible, keep a big space between yourself and people who don't live with you so that we can keep the virus from spreading as quickly.

We may need to make sure the things that come in or out of our homes are cleaned.

You may notice that the grownups who care for you might seem distracted or nervous. It's hard for things to change, even for grownups.

Does it feel strange and different for you to be out of school, or away from the playground, or separated from your friends?

If so, you're not alone. It is strange for most people. Many people all over the world are going through big changes, and some people are very sad or worried. Some people are happy to be home more often. You may feel different ways at different times: and that's normal!

Social distancing is how we can help to care for all the lovable people we know and all the lovable people we don't know.

And remember: this will not last forever!

CPSIA information can be obtained at www.ICGtesting.com
Printed in the USA
BVIW121301260620
582368BV00023B/139